the SMURFS™

LAZY SMURF TAKES A NAP

by Peyo

SIMON SPOTLIGHT
New York   London   Toronto   Sydney   New Delhi
An imprint of Simon & Schuster Children's Publishing Division
1230 Avenue of the Americas, New York, New York 10020
© Peyo - 2012 - Licensed through Lafig Belgium - www.smurf.com. All Rights Reserved.
Originally published in French as *Le Long Sommeil* written by Peyo
English language translation copyright © 2012 by Peyo. All rights reserved.
Translated by Elizabeth Dennis Barton

Manufactured in the United States of America   0512 LAK First Edition 2 4 6 8 10 9 7 5 3 1 ISBN 978-1-4424-4647-2

It was a beautiful summer afternoon in Smurf Village, but most of the Smurfs were too busy doing chores to enjoy it. Lazy Smurf, as usual, was sleeping instead of working. Brainy Smurf lectured Lazy about being a responsible Smurf, but Brainy forgot to watch Papa Smurf's potion while it brewed on the fire, and it burned!

"That potion contained the last of my elm leaves," announced Papa Smurf. "I need to go to the swamp and smurf a new supply. Don't do anything foolish while I'm gone!"

Lazy Smurf yawned. "Now that Papa's gone, I can smurf another nice, long nap!" Then he closed his eyes and fell fast asleep.

Handy Smurf was angry. "He never stops sleeping! Meanwhile we have to smurf all the work," he said. "But I think I know how to teach Lazy a good lesson."

All the Smurfs huddled around to hear Handy's idea.

Much later, Lazy Smurf awoke from a deep sleep. "What a great nap!" he said, stretching. "I think I'll go see what Cook Smurf has smurfed for us to eat."

Back in the village Lazy got quite a shock. Everything in Smurf Village was old and decaying! He saw a fragile old woman weakly trying to water her flowers . . .

When the old woman turned around,
Lazy realized it was Smurfette!

"Lazy Smurf, where have you been?" Smurfette cried. "Three hundred years have passed since you disappeared . . . were you asleep that entire time? And look! You didn't even get older!"

All the other Smurfs came to see him. "It's great to see you," they said. "We are all too old to work. Someone needs to chop wood, smurf the fields, cook . . ."

"But I can't smurf all the work," whined Lazy Smurf. "Where is Papa Smurf?"

"Oh . . . Papa Smurf is no longer with us," the old Smurfs told him, bursting into tears.

"Please don't cry," Lazy Smurf pleaded. "I'll smurf everything I can to help you!"

While the old Smurfs rested, Lazy Smurf worked double time to catch up with the chores. But his two arms just weren't enough.

That night Lazy Smurf collapsed on his bed, completely exhausted. "If only everything could be the way it was before," he wished.

Suddenly he had an idea. He got up and slipped into Papa Smurf's laboratory.

"Aha! Here is what I was looking for!" exclaimed Lazy Smurf, flipping through Papa Smurf's book of spells. "The formula for a youth potion!"

Even though he was exhausted, he gathered all the ingredients together and went right to work.

The next morning Lazy Smurf came in with a big
plate of blue cookies.

"Yum, cookies!" the old Smurfs said. They each grabbed one.

"How are they?" Lazy Smurf asked.

"Hmm . . . they taste a little strange but not bad!" said the old Smurfs.
They ate all the cookies but didn't get any younger.

Lazy Smurf began washing the dishes with a heavy heart. He was thinking about all the chores he was going to have to do, forever, when a bouncy red ball flew through the open window and hit him on the head!

The Smurfs had finally gotten younger, but now they were too young! They had become little children! They ran and giggled and played in the yard.

I will still be stuck doing all the work, Lazy Smurf thought.

Back in the dining room Lazy saw that the table was strewn with fake beards. "They were playing a joke on me!" Lazy Smurf cried. "They weren't old at all. And now I've smurfed them back into little children!"

While Lazy Smurf was thinking about the prank everyone played on him, the curious young Smurfs decided to go on an adventure in the countryside.

Too young to know better, they knocked right on Gargamel's door! The sneaky sorcerer welcomed the young Smurfs inside.

Lazy had followed the young Smurfs and witnessed the entire scene. *This is a catastrophe!* he thought. *But if all this was a trick, that means Papa Smurf must still be alive . . . I must smurf him as fast as I can.*

Lazy ran toward the swamp, hoping to find Papa Smurf there. But Lazy became stuck in the mud, and every time he moved, he sank deeper and deeper!

Suddenly someone grabbed his hand. It was Papa Smurf! He reached down and pulled Lazy from the swamp.

"When I returned to the village, I knew right away something bad had happened," Papa Smurf said.

Lazy told him the whole story, and Papa realized there wasn't a moment to lose. They had to get to Gargamel's house immediately!

Papa and Lazy arrived at Gargamel's house just in time. Gargamel had thrown all the little Smurfs into a big pot. He was going to make Smurf stew! Papa Smurf had an idea.

"Lazy Smurf, listen well to what I am about to tell you," Papa whispered.

Following Papa's instructions, Lazy stretched out on Gargamel's doorstep and began to snore loudly.

"What's that I hear?" cried Gargamel, opening the front door. "There is still one more Smurf!" He plucked up Lazy and threw him in the stew with the others.

Meanwhile, Papa Smurf replaced the spices with an antidote to the youth potion. When Gargamel sprinkled the spices into the stew, the stew exploded and the Smurfs returned to their normal size. While Gargamel stood in shock, they made their escape.

Gargamel didn't have a chance to chase them. He had accidentally swallowed some of the stew and became an old man.

"I need to prepare a youth potion," Gargamel said. "But oh, my aching back!"

"I have learned my lesson," Lazy announced proudly. "I promise to do more work instead of being so lazy. Of course, before I start working, I will need to take a little nap first . . ."